Ho Ho Whoa!
The Tale of Parkour
Santa

For Cameron and James

Published by Attic Wit Press
www.atticwitpress.com

First Printing, 2017

Printed in the United States of America

Ho Ho Whoa!
The Tale of Parkour Santa

Written by Kavae Loseby

Illustrated by Sophia Loseby

and Ella Newman

Everybody knows Christmas
is the most special time of year.

Now there is somebody, somewhere,
who loves Christmas even more than
you and feels Christmas cheer all year
long. His name is Santa Claus, but
you can call him Nick.

Now Nick is always jolly, always
giving and always a saint.

Even better he loves Christmas,
he loves Christmas just the way it is.

Nick loves the sparkly specks of snow
that swirl in the sky. He loves the
warm, spicy taste of Christmas, with
the wintry smells that makes his nose
smile. Most of all he loves the love
that everyone shares.

These things made Christmas special
or so Nick believed. It was perfect, just
right, he would not change a thing,
but it was not up to him.

One year at Christmas a few years ago,
Nick waited and waited and hoped for
some snow. Huge, white clouds
gathered as he held his breath, at last,
at last, but away they went.

That year at Christmas Mrs Claus said,
"No mince pies, no gingerbread, have
a cranberry instead."
"A cranberry Mrs Claus? A cranberry!"
Nick cried. "That's not right at all."

So Nick waited and waited and hoped
some more, for things to turn out like
they did before.

That year at Christmas
like every Christmas before, Nick
called his good friend, his best friend,
the greatest friend of all,
"Come out with me Rudolph for a day
of good cheer."

But Rudolph couldn't come and play.
He had a new family, that included
just three. So Nick waited and waited,
but didn't hope anymore,
for things would never be like they
were before.

For the first time Nick didn't feel very
jolly, or very giving, or like a saint.
Then the worst thing happened
in the whole wide world.

Santa Claus didn't believe in
Santa Claus anymore.

Maybe he was just Nick, good old
Nick, so he took off his Santa coat, his
boots and his hat and went and did
what normal people do on Christmas
Eve, he waited for the magic,
the magic he had lost.

He waited by the mistletoe, wreath
and tinselled tree, but there was just
no magic in the air, or none that he
could see. So he sighed and sighed
and finally said, "I think I'll search
somewhere else instead."

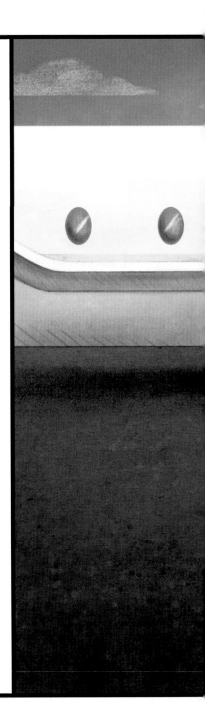

This is nice Nick thought to himself,
as hooves hammered down the
cobbled streets,
nearly as nice as reindeer.

"Whoa!" he cried, "stop here, please."

"Oh no," said the driver. "We can't
stop here, this is Warrior's Walk."

"It's perfect," said Nick, "just right."

What a silly, silly man Nick thought,
as he reached a little park,
with a little bench,
warriors near Paris?

There were warriors, parkour warriors,
who came soaring and bounding,
weaving and climbing, with a dash
vault here and a cat leap there. Then
they stopped and looked Nick's way,
"Joyeux Noël!" they called,

"come and play."

Soon Nick was trying and trying,
but each time he'd fall.

"I'm not doing it right,"
he cried, "not right at all."

"You need a strong spirit,"
the warriors said.

Trying once more Nick held his
breath, at last, at last, away he went,
leaping and bounding,
weaving and climbing.

Then Nick wondered and wondered
and thought some more, things don't
need to be like they were before.
I'll be a new Nick with new tricks up
my sleeve, in Parkour Santa
I just have to believe.

Soon, it was time for the warriors to
go their own way and wait for the
magic of Christmas Day. Nick realised
they were waiting and waiting
and hoping for him.

They believed he would come
and come he would.

So Nick hurried home, put on his
parkour hoodie, his special sneakers
and sack and with a Jingle Bells Jump
and a Fa-La-La Flip he went and did
what Parkour Santa does on
Christmas Eve, what Parkour Santa
does best.

He went and shared the magic.

"HO HO WHOA!"

On that certain Christmas Day,
it did not snow, not one speck, but
Parkour Santa simply said,
"I'll do something else to make it
special instead."

On that certain Christmas Day,
Mrs Claus baked no gingerbread, but
Parkour Santa simply said,
"I'll eat something else, a special
cranberry instead."

On that certain Christmas Day,
Rudolph couldn't come and play, but
Parkour Santa simply said,
"I'll come and help you out instead."

Christmas was special after all.

Everybody knows Christmas is the
most special time of year,
there is a certain something,
a special magic in the air.
But there is a secret, a secret that
Parkour Santa knows.

We put the magic there.

Made in the USA
Middletown, DE
08 February 2019